#66 87

P-M
May

Mayer, Mercer.
Just me and my
puppy

DATE DUE   PERMA-BOUND

DE 15 '89	MY 18 '93	MAY 0 5 2006
	AE 28 '94	MAY 1 9 2006
JA 16 '90	OC 19 '94	
AP 17 '90		FEB 1 6 2011
MY 08 '90	AB 27	
AP 8 '91	NOV 27 '00	
SE 30 '91		
	DEC 18 '00	
FE 14 '92	JAN 9 01	
FE 27 '92	FEB 0 3 2005	
MR 5 92	OCT 2 8 2005	
AP 20 '93	NOV 1 4 2005	
AP 30 '93	JAN 1 3 2006	
	JAN 1 3 2006	

JUST ME AND MY PUPPY

BY
MERCER MAYER

A GOLDEN BOOK • NEW YORK
Western Publishing Company, Inc., Racine, Wisconsin 53404

I wanted a puppy, just for me.
So I traded my baseball mitt for one.

My baby sister liked him
right away.

And, boy, were Mom and Dad surprised!
They said I could keep him if I took
care of him myself.

So I am taking very good care
of my puppy.
I feed him in the morning.

He eats every bite.

Then I put on his leash and
we go for a walk.

I am teaching my puppy
how to heel.

He is learning how to stay . . .

. . . except when he sees a cat.

My puppy knows lots of tricks . . .

how to sit . . .

how to play dead . . .

. . . and how to roll over.

He still needs some practice.

But he already knows how to fetch.

My puppy is a big help around the house.

He's a good guard dog.

He brings in
the paper
for my dad.

And he keeps me company
while I do my homework.

Sometimes my puppy gets dirty.

Then I give him a bath.

I get him nice and dry
so he won't catch a cold.

Then we get ready for bed . . .

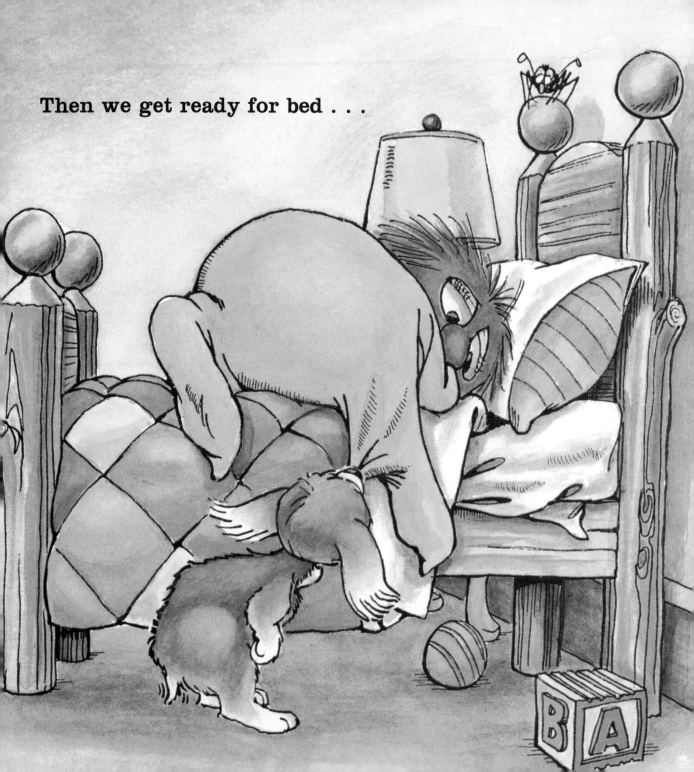

. . . just me and my puppy.